YOU ARE A
Beautiful
BEGINNING

WRITTEN BY

NINA LADEN

ILLUSTRATED BY

KELSEY GARRITY-RILEY

Roaring Brook Press

New York

It is not the number of pages.

It is the story in the book.

It is not how far you traveled.

It is the journey that you took.

It is not remembering the lyrics.

It is singing a song in your heart.

It is not creating a masterpiece.

It is finding the courage to start.

It is not about winning the game.

It is having fun while you play.

It is not making the most friends.

It is loving the one who is there.

It is not owning everything.

It is bringing something to share.

It is not being a hero.

It is being part of a team.

It is not putting up walls.

It is about building a dream.

It is not hogging the sunshine.

It is helping others to grow.

It is not being afraid of darkness.

It is looking for places that glow.

It is not wishing to be different.

It is learning to love being you.

It is not the end of your story.

It is a beautiful beginning, too.

For Brenda Winter Hansen—a beautiful friend

—N. L.

For Llewyn, at the beginning

—K. G. R.

Text copyright © 2020 by Nina Laden
Illustrations copyright © 2020 by Kelsey Garrity-Riley
Published by Roaring Brook Press
Roaring Brook Press is a division of Holtzbrinck Publishing Holdings Limited Partnership
120 Broadway, New York, NY 10271
mackids.com

Library of Congress Cataloging-in-Publication Data is available
ISBN 978-1-250-31183-2

Our books may be purchased in bulk for promotional, educational, or business use. Please contact your local
bookseller or the Macmillan Corporate and Premium Sales Department at (800) 221-7945 ext. 5442 or by email at
MacmillanSpecialMarkets@macmillan.com.

First edition, 2020
Book design by Cassie Gonzales
Printed in China by RR Donnelley Asia Printing Solutions Ltd.,
Dongguan City, Guangdong Province

The illustrations in this book were created with gouache, ink, and colored pencils, with a little bit of digital editing.

1 3 5 7 9 10 8 6 4 2